In   of

the Bear

Ewan Lawrie

Non

Non-U/KDP

Contents

4 Word Foreword

This could be true.

In the Mouth of the Bear

CHARLOTTENBURG,

Wilmersdorf,

Kanstrasse,

Ku'dorf.

The usual places could be chanted like a children's learning rhyme.

Pink and garish neon, mulberry-stained dawns and drink. So much drink. And, naturally, all artificial light was obscured by dense and pungent tobacco smoke. Unwise liaisons, broken hearts - on both sides of the cultural divide. We wore our rebellion as a uniform, before donning the real thing to go to work.

The best of times? Maybe... And the worst? Maybe that too...

The City of the Bear: two cities in one, Siamese twins conjoined at the heart by concrete and watchtowers. Yin - the grey capital of a corrupt and dying regime, Yang - the glitzy whore's heart of mostly upbeat –isms; capitalism, hedonism and dubious sexual tourism. One year to go to Orwell's dystopian vision; who knew it would turn out like this? In six short years all the certainties of the Cold War would start to crumble: they'd applied the Domino Theory to the wrong game.

How exciting! You say. City of spies, escapes and drama. Did you know? Could you tell the twilight was coming? And the answer is no, how could I? It was all numbers and databases, trends, peaks and troughs: statistics, not dead-letter drops, honey traps and exchanges of spies on neutral ground. And we were young, early 20s or younger – interested in birds, bands and booze; pockets full of money. Deliberately overpaid to help us flout our conspicuous consumption in front of the Soviets and the fuming Ostberliners: Propagandist Party Animals.

There was a train. If you didn't drive -and wouldn't fly- it was how you got from West Berlin to West Germany. The Berlin Military Train: several coaches and a large dining car. We used to board at 0800 hours: by

9 we had started on the canned beer. The locomotive would be changed after the checkpoint on the edge of West Berlin: an East German engine pulled you all the way to Magdeburg. Lunch and wine from a very good cellar was served as the Duty Train Officer handed all the Berlin Travel Documents to a Soviet Captain in full dress uniform on the platform. Someone likely to have queued for potatoes at a butcher's watched us swilling the red and chomping our steak, no wonder he pretended to dot every incomprehensible i and cross every non-cyrillic t. The Berlin Military Train travelled daily.

So no, I didn't feel the hand of history: we drank, danced and debauched for 10 years and were as self-important as any twenty-somethings have any right to be. And yet... we were spied upon, by untrained fellow servicemen: our own mini-STASI on the wrong side of the wall.

But what a time it was. What a city. Berliners knew it and wouldn't hesitate to tell you so. It was a magnet for draft dodgers, alternative lifestyles and sexual outcasts. No wonder Bowie had moved there for a few years. How fitting it was that the City of the Bear nestled like a stale blini in the mouth of the Russian Bear, we were closer to Warsaw than Hamburg.

So this is a flavour of our Berlin; not much Realpolitik, no espionage secrets and no I-told-you-so analysis: just young people, away from home, with too much money and not quite enough sense.

2

Weather Report

I'D BEEN SENT UP on the roof to do a weather recce. They did that to all the new people,

'Get the keys, Airman' – or Airwoman, it was 1982 – 'up on the roof, take a pencil and paper. We need a weather report. Are those Sovs going to fly to-day or not? Your stand-down depends on it.'

The officer handed me a pair of binos. I nodded and kept my smirk inside. I snatched a log-pad from one of the 'live' positions. Jock was just about to insert the carbons and fill in the headers, he shouted 'Hey!' and I told him to fuck off.

It was a really beautiful day. The sky was as blue as the underside of a Mig-25. To the north I could see a faint contrail dissipating, ready to fool people into believing it was a mare's tail cloud. From the rooftop, between the giant globes and the phallus which gave the listening station its nickname, you could see the whole of the city. East and West. All the tit-for-tat landmarks, like the Funkturm and its Ostberliner counterpart. I fancied I could see the Brandenburg and the wide avenue of Unter den Linden on the other side. Perhaps I could, although I couldn't foresee a time when I would ever walk down it.

The wind was blowing from the east. I was on the highest hill in the city. The Americans had bulldozed ruins into a big pile and put Teufelsberg listening post on it just after the war. A phallic salute to the Russians who had almost beaten the Allies to Berlin. I looked down and saw the green, luscious Grünewald. My first trip up to work had been disrupted by a wild boar running in front of the shift bus. We'd just passed the Grunewald S-Bahn station when it ran out of the forest. I'd been thinking about Platform 17 and the hundreds and thousands who left for Auschwitz without a return ticket. I scanned for the S-Bahn with the binos. Then I did a 360, stopping at Wannsee, watching one of a cruise boat crew mopping and cleaning the decks for another day showing the tourists round beautiful Berlin. My boat trip had been 2 days after my arrival since I'd taken my embarkation leave at the business end. The guide didn't point out the beautiful building on Am Großen Wannsee where the Final Solution had been drily debated like some Pan-European economic policy.

The binoculars swung to the Mercedes Building, over by the Blue Church and I felt a shiver not entirely due to the wind.

Later, I took a seat on a concrete block. I filled 10 pages of the log pad with the longest weather reconnaissance report I could come up with. Eventually someone – a Corporal, just in case, I think – was sent up to bring me down.

'Finished?' He asked.

'Yes, Corporal!' I replied.

He blushed, he was no older than I was.

We returned to the set room. Nothing much was going on. I gave the officer my report.

He started to laugh, but stopped suddenly when he realised he couldn't read the Russian.

3

Nightclubbing

I LOOKED MADAME STRADIVARIUS in the eye and grinned. A slight lift at the corner of her mouth and then the naked violinist carried on with her act.

'Beers?' Dave enquired, already seated, eyes glued to the curtain-covered door to the left of the stage.

'What else?' said Jock, as I gave a nod and sat down. Opposite Dave, my back to the stage.

The waitress turned up with the beers before we ordered though; the short hair and British accents making her mind up: saving time. Her time was still money, though she was past working as a hostess here in Mon Cheri's. A Kabarett – Cabaret in English, if you like: but you'd be hard pushed to picture Liza with a Zee here. It was dark except for the Klieg Lights lighting the tiny stage. Four people might fit on it, if they were very close together – which they sometimes were.

Mon Cheri was the name of a hideous brand of liqueur chocolate that the Germans were crazy about. One of the girls did a show every night that gave the club its name: Madame Stradivarius wasn't the only novelty act in here. We called it Mons: linguists like word play.

I took a sip of the beer. The grimace on Dave and Jock's faces had told me it was Charlottenburger Pils... the only beer available in these places seemingly. At 10 Deutschmarks a throw it cost roughly 20 times a NAAFI beer. As Jock liked to say, you expect to pay something for the ambulance. The Paganini tape over the PA was approaching the end. Birgitte would soon be off stage. Dave craned his neck for a better view of the curtain. Jock scanned the room, checking out the clientele.

' Two "Gee I's" at 2 o'clock' he said.

' A schnapps says they leave with assistance.' I laughed

'I'll no take that bet, thanks.' I hadn't expected him to. Dave was still mooning at that curtain. We didn't call them 'Gee I's' because they were military –

although they probably were. Birgitte was taking her bow on-stage, and her *bow* off it. Right on cue a very loud voice rang out:

'Gee I never seen that in Kansas!'

Only the state varied, but they all said it - all of them. The trick was having a suitable comment on the state. Some nights that was easier than others:

'Too right, Toto' we chorussed, even Dave. I felt a hand on my shoulder, the smell of 'Poison': a football stadium perfume: overpowering in Mons and unmistakable.

'Ah, Schmetterling. Is tonight the night?' It was a joke. She always called me Butterfly: I wasn't sure why.

'Not tonight 'Gitte, I've got the clap.'

'Schmetti, you can't cut your finger if you don't use the knife! Come on, tonight, with me. A special price.'

I expect I was neither first nor last to hear this on that particular night. In any case she was still joking. I never touched the women in any of the clubs, as Birgitte well knew.

'Ach, Schmetti, I'll see you in five minutes... you can buy me champagne!'

'Two things 'Gitte: it's not champagne and the other business would be cheaper!' I smiled at that.

'Exactly, Schmetterling, exactly'. Her returning smile seemed genuine, and she and the fiddle headed off through Dave's curtain.

The champagne was a bigger scam than the beer. The bottle would arrive already opened in a bucket of ice, 15 minutes after ordering. It takes time to pour in the Babycham and water it down. The price - of course - was more ridiculous than the taste. The way to play the game was to agree to buy a piccolo; a pencil thin glass of the same concoction at 15 marks a go. This guaranteed customers thirty minutes of the ladies' time, if you were well behaved.

I lifted my pilsner.

' Here's to the running dogs of capitalism!'

' Saving the world for democracy!' Jock returned.

' CND forever!' said Dave, a crooked smile on his face.

The beers clinked above the bottle-scarred table:

' Fuck 'em!' we saved sincerity 'til last, as usual.

Dave turned towards Jock: taking the curtain –and the stage out of his eye-line. Ute must have gone on stage. Sure enough; 'Lola' started on the PA. There was nothing special about Ute's act, until the end that is. She did a mostly straightforward strip act. Dave started:

'I've got my interview next week, you know...'

'So? The usual lies is it?' Jock sniggered at my question.

'I'm no' your referee, am I?'

'No, he is, as usual... just' Dave replied.

'What? You want me to tell the truth this time?' I broke in.

It was gratifying to watch the beer jet out of Jock's nostrils.

'Actually, you'd better. I'm going to, you see.'

'Dinna be daft!' Jock was shocked, not laughing now.

'You know what that means, don't you?' He knew and I knew, everyone did.

'A one-way ticket out. Out of Berlin, out of the RAF. I don't care.'

Jock and I looked at each other, hoping the drink was talking, thinking for the first time about returning to base, even at this early hour. Dave got up, went to the toilet. Always did, during Ute's act.

'Got it bad.' Jock announced.

'As could be' I allowed. I raised my eyebrows at Jock. He shrugged.

'No' our business, really!'

I sighed. That wasn't good enough.

Dave was Ute's Mr Goodbar. She didn't have to go looking for him. On days off Dave would be in his seat, waiting for the club to close. He'd look away when she was on-stage; when shadowy figures followed her through the curtain. Later Ute and Dave would go off into the dawn. He'd arrive back at base two days later, to get changed for work.

We never thought it would get serious. Ute's act proved that they couldn't get married, not even in Berlin. I had assumed the novelty would wear off. Things looked bad for Jock and me: if Dave confessed all, we couldn't admit we knew - and if we couldn't prove we didn't - the end would be the same. We'd be out the door too, seconds behind Dave.

The piccolo and Birgitte arrived at the same time. She made no acknowledgement of the aging waitress. Maybe she saw her own future in the poster paint make up and the lined, defeated face.

'So, Schmetti, where is Philip?' Never Phil.

'The laser beam smile snagged a Dutch air hostess in the Harp... Hours ago, you know Phil'. I wondered if she'd get any of that.

' The tart's off wi' another wan, he means' said Jock helpfully.

'Ach, Philip, he is bad for business... or those girls are.' She said bitterly.

'Gitte…' I began. 'About Ute and Dave…' She looked at me hard. Then:

'Ja, Schmetti, you are right. It is time. For a while now. It is just…

She was so happy, Schmetti. …' She had a distant look.

Birgitte was beautiful in either profile. But the God of Symmetry had played a cruel joke: Birgitte in full face would never make it in the Dream Factory. Not even Beate Uhse could use her was her bitter joke for the Brits; connoisseurs of the porno video one and all. Not ugly, of course: just … well… startlingly asymmetrical.

'So, 'Gitte… what…?' My question petered out.

'Don't worry. I'll take care of it. It isn't the first time, you know?'

She gave a twisted smile, tossed off her fake drink and went over to the Kansas farmboys: time *is* money.

Ute gave up her secret during Ray Davies' fade out: A predictable Midwestern twang rang out. I expect there aren't many transsexual strippers in Topeka. Ute was running for the curtained door when Birgitte shouted:

'Ute, here! These boys need company, come on! We're short tonight'

Ute looked round. Looking for Dave, who was still in the bog. She wrapped a diaphanous skirt round herself and reluctantly sat down. Dave's girl didn't do much of the hostess bit. The customers who followed her through the curtain were a niche market. They had come to Mons in search of Ute. They had no need to be persuaded over drinks, fake or not.

Ute sat next to the 'Gee I' with the bone haircut. A marine from the US Embassy guard force probably. Six feet three of meathead.

' Telt ye it wasna worth a bet!' said the laconic Jock.

Dave came out. Looked at the empty stage. Clocked Ute with the Marine: she shook her head. Dave came and sat down.

'What's that about?' Almost petulant.

'Gitte says they're short tonight.' I said. 'Flu. All the girls in town are getting it.' '

' Elephant Bar's closed: first time since the wall went up.' Jock added helpfully.

The haggard waitress wheeled a bucket up to the Yanks' table. Open bottle poking out of a mountain of ice. There was a sort of smile on her face: one that would scare children. I hadn't seen the Americans order the drink. Birgitte poured everyone a drink. Looking cheerfully manic she raised her glass. Ute brought hers up slower, looking over at Dave...

Who was taking it badly.

'Look I know, right. It's business. And the men that come, you know, looking for her. Well it's different, that's all - sitting with customers. *Talking* to them.'

I shot Jock a look. Hoped he would say nothing. Poor Dave. Trying so hard not to be jealous.

I signalled to the bar. Three more beers. They came:

'And schnapps, Persico, dreimal', holding up three redundant fingers to the waitress.

'Dave, it's the job. Alright?'

'Yeah, well...' And he took a long slug of beer.

Three Persico arrived. The schnapps was banned in West Germany; reputedly it had aphrodisiac qualities. It was powerful. It was sweet. And it was effective at removing inhibitions. Dave downed his almost before the glasses touched the table top. I pushed mine toward him.

' Have it, I don't feel like it... tonight.'

It went the same way. Jock kicked me under the table. I gave him a long stare. He shrugged.

'Ha'e mines too, Dave.'

Jurgen, the boss, came out from behind the curtain. Short -stocky to his face, fat behind his back – he didn't look scary. We knew better. 2 of 3 Para's finest had been hospitalised a few weeks ago: fair enough, you don't damage the girls. A look flashed between him and Birgitte. I thought I could see him raise his eyebrows: he'd noticed Ute. Meathead was animated now: pointing at the champagne, shaking his head. Shouting. Jurgen bowled over.

'A problem, gentlemen?'-

Nothing on stage, no music: an expectant hush.

'Damn' right sir! Ain't payin' for it. Didn't ask for it!'

'But did you drink it, sir?' His politeness would have scared me.

'Hell, yeah! But... you know, we thought it was free!'

'And these ladies are in love with you, of course.'

Meathead's face fell at Jurgen's words. He'd been a fool. We all knew it, even him now.

So it kicked off. Meathead and his sidekick lunged over the table at Jurgen. Naturally, he was too quick for a couple of drunks. They sprawled on the floor. Jurgen was first in with the boots, before the reinforcements materialised. Two of the customers weren't. Sometimes the heavies sat at the tables. Pour encourager les autres, you might say. It wasn't an epic battle. The victors dragged the defeated outside, while Jurgen 'phoned his contact in the Military Police over at Templehof.

Ute had looked terrified throughout. Not used to the rough and tumble of the tables. Dave tried to stop her as she made for the curtain and safety out the back. No luck. He sat down miserably. Birgitte winked at me.

'Drinks for my friends! Here, this table.'

The waitress didn't merit even a name. Birgitte sat next to Dave. Hand on his thigh.

' Don't worry, Dave. She will be OK, 100%. Just leave her, hey?'

'But...'

He was cut short as Birgitte rammed a Persico to his lips and poured it down him.

'You'll feel better in a minute, Dave. Sure will.'

She jerked her head at me, waved with the spare hand at the empty table to the left. I finally returned Jock's kick under the table. Jabbed a thumb to show him the way. We took our beers. Left the schnapps.

It was horrible. Watching a professional at work. On one of us. Our first night in here, months ago, had drawn the battle lines. We weren't ordinary mugs. Our eyes were open and we were in here on our terms. A bucket arrived. And more schnapps. Ute came out after an hour or so. Sat at the bar. Trying not to watch. I saw a tear as Birgitte led Dave behind the curtain.

Jock and I went up to the bar. Piled everything from our wallets on the bar.

'For Dave's bill' I said.

Jurgen appeared behind us, a hand on my shoulder, a hand on Jock's.

'No charge' he said. 'What are friends for?'

'We'll pay, thanks.' And we did.

But we knew we owed him anyway.

4

Elephant

'I 'LL NEVER FORGET THE **night the Elephant flew in to Berlin Zoo**', Bill declared. We'd all been silent for a few minutes; a round dozen of forty-or–sos (or a dozen of round forty-somethings) a few drinks showing on the judgement-ometer. All the awkward questions over, we knew who was still married to whom and who had finally come out. It was time to hear the old stories again. Tales from a city split by barbed wire and bricks: West Berlin had been all colour, while the East was as monochrome as the earnest films they allowed out into the world. We'd lived through it, the Cold War in the spy capital of the world. Seen the wall come down, watched the graffiti spread like eczema on formerly pristine Berlin walls. It had been an incredible time. And Bill would never forget the delivery of an elephant.

We had listened, more than watched, as the Cold War eventually thawed. Like the slush in the streets, it was messy. We professional eavesdroppers worked on the top of Berlin's only hill; Teufelsberg, Devil's Mountain; a grand name for little more than a hillock. Built from the post-war rubble even as the city was being dismembered by the four "allied" powers, the Americans wasted no time in establishing a listening post on the top. By the early Eighties, an engineer with a sense of humour had erected the structure known to the Berliners as "Der Pimmel auf der Himmel", the Prick in the Sky.

All through the Eighties, we listened and listened, trying to piece together the intelligence puzzle. What were they capable of? Could they get 500 tanks to Hamburg, Bonn and Frankfurt in a day? Could they launch a strategic nuclear missile from an aircraft based just south of Berlin. Nobody was sure. So every report was a "possible indication of a possible incidence of a probable impossibility." It was so vague. It was all a game. Bluffing on a scarcely credible scale. Or so it proved. The missiles in the silos didn't work. We had heard the rumours of Soviet incompetence before glasnost's arrival . Why would their armed forces be more efficient?

But no, we did our bit; we kept intelligence budgets high to fight a horde of shadow boxers.

There was some excitement, Bill's unforgettable elephant.

'**да слон на борту**' 'Confirmed, Elephant on board'

The stamping of feet, raised voices,

'Don't be ridiculous, you're not taking this seriously! We are not reporting that!'

And we didn't. But the rest room was full the next evening to watch the East German TV news, and the arrival of the elephant at Berlin Zoo via the Glienicke Bridge, like an exchanged spy.

5

International Relations

NADA FINISHED POLISHING THE glass. Shook the cloth in Phil's face. It would have been a playful gesture a week ago, before he'd met her daughter. Phil's grin was glued in place by a gallon of Warsteiner beer and Yugoslavian schnapps. The lights were dim in Nada's: the pink-lettered neon outside said 'Treffpunkt' at the front and 'Meeting Point' on the side. Nada's could be found deep in the Ku'damm Eck, an indoor drinking precinct, with the odd shop. On the Kurfurstendamm; maybe it's still there.

It had been a funny night in Nada's: Julischka, her daughter was out of bounds for chit-chat, now. No point in asking about Nada's latest man. Her last romantic adventure was also a no-go area. There hadn't been much else to talk about. As usual, all the other custom had been casual: people may have met here, but few stayed. Except us.

It was after five: the last of the electro-pop had been played on the bar's cheap stereo; Howard Jones had given way to reels and wailing from somewhere round Zagreb. It was the signal to drink up and leave, bat-blind in the dawn. Unless, of course, you were favoured guests, foot up on the rail at the Stammtisch.

'Reckon we'd better go...' I said jerking my head towards Phil.

'Aye, he's cocked it up alright... haha...' Jock slurred a little.

'Very funny: I'm surprised she let us use the table.'

' You're no' wrong. Phil's awfy gubbed, eh?'

'Feeling guilty, I bet'.

I asked for the bill. Only in Berlin; a rootless Brit speaking fractured German to a Yugoslavian emigrée. She'd be a Bosnian Serb nowadays. Berlin was full of 'Balkan' restaurants, Yugoslav run bars -and clip-joints. Phil had complained one night in the Elephant Bar before the cabaret; a whore had hit him, he'd said, to a very large man with a shaven head and a silver-coloured front tooth. What you do? The man had asked, his English as good as his German. Nothing, nothing, Phil had protested, I only asked her what part of Balkania she was from. Maybe the heavy'd just decided against beating someone already brain-damaged; he'd given an angry growl and thrown all of us out.

Nada offered one for the road; a Bismarck. A powerful schnapps she saved for special occasions. Like Phil's birthday, six months ago.

The big galoot had got comatose on it: Nada had taken him home. Next days off, in the early evening, I'd asked her what went on.

'Nichevo, nichts, nothing' the smile had spread across her face, making her look 30-ish - not forty something.

'What? What's the joke?'

'First the British sink the Bismarck... then the Bismarck sink the British!'

She'd exploded with laughter. Tears rolling; the years falling off her as they did. She was an attractive woman; twenty years older than all of us; me, Jock and Phil. The offer of a schnapps for the road seemed genuine.

Maybe Phil hadn't queered the pitch after all. Nada's brown eyes were blackly unreadable in the crepuscular gloom of the bar. I accepted the drinks for all of us.

'He's had enough! Just you.' She hissed.

Phil didn't notice. The grin stayed, but he wasn't there. His body could have followed his mind and left us with the Cheshire teeth gleaming. Nada's lips were taut, every movement was accompanied by a toss of her black hair. Glasses clattered onto the shelves. Her heels machine gunned across the tiles behind the bar. I knew where she was aiming.

We should all have named Nada as a 'foreign contact'. Any foreign national you met more than once had to be declared to the correct authorities. I'd never have had time to go to work. Anyway, checking up on us gave the men in the sports jackets and brogues something to do. While they missed the real spies in the next door office at the base headquarters. Jock eyed this one last drink warily, as if suspecting a mickey. That was ludicrous; we were on the Ku'damm not in Kreuzberg. I raised my glass.

'Zdorovye, Nada!' I tossed it off in the Slavic style, pretended to throw the glass, before carefully setting it on the copper bar-top. She didn't return the toast. Unusual, but not unexpected in the circumstances.

'Let us buy you something, Nada.' I suggested.

'You'll take a whiskey, aye!' said Jock, who never touched the stuff. 'You've the Talisker away up there.' Thereby proving he could read and bluff at the same time.

Jock was always the most reluctant to leave this bar. After the night of Phil's birthday he hadn't spoken to him for a week. It had been quiet in his car on the way to work. I'd felt like a SALT talks interpreter, a go-between for the irreconcilable.

'Take him home,' she couldn't say his name.

'Of course we will'. We chorused, anxious to placate.

'Don't come back, not with him.'

She hawked, and spat with vigour on the gleaming copper, in front of the oblivious Phil.

6

Error of Judgement

'WE'RE KNACKERED, NOW!' I said, out of breath. Doc rolled his eyes, unable to reply, busy heaving in a huge gulp of air, purple with exertion. And why not? It's hard to run after fifteen hours on the toot, as he so quaintly called it. He was dressed as usual according to the Border Farmer's Template #2 : Dances, informal dinners and meetings at the bank. That is, stout brogues, twill and Harris Tweed jacket. Not a common look in the fleshpots of Berlin, I admit.

We were knackered. Stuffed, stymied, stiffed or just plain fucked, if you prefer. The concrete wall at the end of our blind alley truly marked it as a dead end. Our pursuers hadn't yet followed us in, but they would.

'What the hell did you say to him, eh?' Not that it mattered, the tall figure had taken the worst kind of offence.

'I only asked him if he got fed up of ruining his tights on the bristles on his legs!'

Doc seemed to think this a perfectly reasonable question. And it might have been... On neutral ground; the Hofbrauhaus opposite the Zoo, say, or the Irish Bar in the Europa Centre. But we hadn't been on neutral ground. Ranke Drei, the Warsteiner Pub had kicked out at two a.m. We hadn't had too much to drink then, since we'd left under our own steam with only a few expletives to help us on our way. Friendly ones that is; Adriana, behind the bar, had once gone out with a Royal Welch Fusilier from Mountain Ash and the only English she could remember was 'Fuck off, you English bastards'. Useful in the valleys I suppose. So, at 2.15 we'd had a choice; a taxi ride to Charlottenburg and ten marks a beer, or nip further off the beaten track into the bars on the sidestreets off the Ku'damm and Uhlandstrasse. We'd been in a few of these before, and, well, if we didn't find precisely the one we wanted, we'd stumble on another.

'Shall we no get a taxi, then?' Doc said. Not a big fan of exercise, we hadn't seen a light in an hour of walking.

' Look, we're bound to find one in a minute... turn left here.'

I looked up at the street sign; 'Katzen-jammerstrasse' it looked like. We took the turn. About fifty yards down was a violent splash of pink neon: 'Finger-hutte' it read.

'What's it called?' asked Doc.

'It means 'Thimbles'.' I replied.

What sort of name for a pub is that?'

'It's a good name for one that's still open.' I said.

It had about five metres of frontage, so I reckoned they were saving a lot on rates. The sign was as wide as the pub. The window looked very dark. There was a priest's hole arrangement on the door. We knocked.

'Are you open?' I asked, in pigeon German.

'Of course.' A shaved moustachioed head looked us both up and down. 'Are you sure you want to come in?'

'Of course we are. I'm gagging for a drink.' Doc told him.

The lights inside reflected off the gatekeeper's pate as he bent to draw back the bolts. Doc gave me a relieved grin and a thumbs up as he barged past on his way to the bar.

'Have you ordered yet?' I asked him after a hard fight to get alongside him.

''course I have. Two beers.' He smiled proudly at me.

'You weren't asked if you'd prefer a snowball?'

'What are you on about?'

'Just look around the bar, Doc. Don't kick off, just take a look.'

He looked. Then he looked like he'd stepped into a bar on another planet.

'Its... we're... ' he couldn't even say it.

I put my hand on his arm.

'Yeah, that's right. Listen, what we're going to do is...' ' drink our beer, speak when we're spoken to, pay the bill, leave a good tip and go, alright?'

He nodded slowly, like a serious child.

It was a small operation. The shaven headed biker-type was doing duty as the only barman. He nodded at me, maybe he was saying I'd handled the situation ok. The clientele was quite subdued; maybe that was our fault. The music was playing at a civilised level for conversation; Erasure, Andy and Vince churning out electro-pop. I felt sorry for Doc: I don't expect there were many places like this in Galashiels, not in 1984 at least.

Inevitably, someone came up to try their luck. Jacket and tie, fashionably cut he looked like a lawyer or a banker. He spoke immaculate English:

'Your first time here?' he raised an eyebrow at me.

'Yep, a mutual friend has played a joke on us...' I gestured at Doc and shrugged.

'Ah... you won't be staying, then?'

'We'll finish our beer if that's ok?'

'Of course, my name is Kurt. I am the owner, please have another drink and then by all means take your leave.'

He smiled, I expect this wasn't the first time, someone had blundered in by mistake. Kurt held two fingers up to the biker and made his retreat.

I was starting to think we would depart with our dignity - and the other customers' – intact. Doc drained the last of his second beer. I winked at Kurt and headed for the exit. I stepped round a tall woman. And Doc didn't. I was half way out the door. Turning, I saw an amicable conversation... until a large meaty hand slapped Doc's face. I went back grabbed his arm and frog-marched him out. The door slammed behind us. We stood under the street light, I was too angry to speak. The door opened, Kurt and the tall woman came out shouting

'Hey, wait...!

But we were already running.

'This way, it's this way. Two left turns and we'll be on the Kanstrasse, in the light and in the traffic, come on.'

We ran. I was wrong. So we were waiting by overflowing skips, in front of a concrete wall, in a dead-end street.

'Ready for a kickin' then?' asked Doc.

'Have to be, won't we?'

Kurt and the woman appeared at the alley mouth. I could see Doc tense up.

'You really must be more careful, gentlemen!' said Kurt, as he handed Doc his wallet.

7

Come and Join the Fun

O N THE RADIO, HEAVEN 17 were going to live for a very long time. I
didn't think I would. I'd spent the day
on 'Racks': changing the tapes in 90
cassette recorders every 20 minutes. I
leaned against the side of the car and
closed my eyes.

Nothing I hadn't seen before on
Teufelseestrasse, no point in looking
out the window. Phil was driving; Paddy was in front; Dave was on Orderly
Corporal, in the guardroom back at

the station. I stretched out, as much as you can in the back of a Beetle. It was Christmas Eve: snow lined the road in greying piles. Full cloud cover promised more snow. The roads were quiet. Most Berliners would be at home enjoying Weinacht, the streets would be busy later: people going to Midnight Mass.

We negotiated the Scholzplatz dash: two traffic lights exactly 220 metres apart. If you completed the dash in 10 seconds at 80 kmh, you beat all the lights along 5 km length of the Heer-strasse. The speed limit was 50. The RMP pulled us over by the BP garage:

' No low flying here, Corporal,' the Redcap said to Phil.

' Yeah sorry, mate, just finished work.' He was offhand.

' I'm going to let you off, mate, I didn't think you RAF types were so keen. You're heading back to an exercise on Gatow, sonny. Mind how you go.'

He smirked and sent us on our way.

'Bollocks.' Paddy was really plosive on the B, I wiped my cheek. 'You reckon he was winding us up,or what?'

'Who fucking knows?' I said. 'Let's just drive by the camp gates, if there's a queue, there's an exercise on. And we'll drive past and have a quiet drink in Kladow.'

'QDIK. Brilliant!' Paddy banged out the B even harder.

The queue started about 2 km from the main and only access gate. Another car from the shift was in front of us:

the Polish section, all of it, fitted into a mini. Any stand-downs and it fitted on a push-bike. I was just glad I hadn't taken the shift bus to work.

'Which pub?' Paddy wanted to know.

'One that's open,' Phil offered. 'It's Christmas Eve, we'll be lucky.'

'What about the Hof?' I suggested.

'Kladower or Gatower?' said Paddy.

'You mong! We're heading towards Kladow aren't we!' I jeered.

We abandoned the car in the Dia supermarket car park. Light seeped out of the Kladower Hof's dingy windows, the dusty net-curtains holding it back as much as the dirty panes. Paddy gave the door a good shove and we spilled into the bar.

The RMP from the garage was sitting on one of the benches. He had his arm round Martina, who lived up the road. She was fat, but people said she was keen. The Redcap nodded and said,

'Get 'em in then.'

8

Mustapha's Taxi

THE TAXI-DRIVER'S HEAVILY ACCENT-
ED German was difficult to un-
derstand. I tried English.

'Mustapha's, off Giesebeckstrasse,
please, mate.'

'Ah. English. Mustapha's is good
name for restaurant, yes.'

At least that meant he'd heard of it.
Doc was blootered in the back seat
saying

'Geez A Break Strasse' and giggling.
Probably still relieved at our narrow

escape after our visit to Thimbles. We needed some food right enough.

'My friend, sorry. Is it open the Mustapha's?'

'What time is it? I asked.

'3.55.'

'That's ok, just need to be at a table before 5.30 a.m.'

I shoved Doc over to the other side of the back seat. The snores were deafening in my right ear. The driver wasn't Turkish, I knew that much. It was unusual that it wasn't a German though. I couldn't remember the last time a 'foreigner' had been behind the wheel of one of the big cream Mercedes taxis.

'You're a long way from home, eh?' I ventured. He could answer, or not. His choice.

'Yes, my friend. Further than you think.' An intriguing answer, had he meant it to be? No chance of repartee with Doc at the moment, so I said:

'But you don't know what I think, do you?'

'OK, my friend, you guess where I come from, you don't pay. You don't guess, pay double meter, yes?' It was a 10-minute ride, how could I lose?

The driver was olive skinned, the five-o-clock shadow looked like nearing the second time around, although I'd have bet he'd shaved before coming on shift. He was about 30. He wore a collarless, white shirt, a cheap if well-cared for suit. Every so often he would smile and a gold tooth would glint in the street lighting or the car headlamps. I could not for the life of me place his accent; he could have been born anywhere from Khartoum to Kazakhstan. He smiled.

'My name is Mustapha too. I will help you. You can ask me questions, except for the obvious ones, OK?'

It seemed fair enough.

'Are you a Muslim?' No use beating about the bush, I thought.

'Well, yes, I am.'

'Did you learn to drive in your home country?' I admit it, I was quite drunk too.

He laughed.

'Yes, we have roads and everything.'

'And how long have you been in Berlin?'

I was hoping to catch him out somehow.

'I have been here 2 years I left... well I left home in 1982.'

Almost, I thought.

'And do you have a visa. A permit.' I sounded like the police.

'I am here legally.' He wasn't fazed.

'Why?' Well, I might as well find out something about him, I thought.

He sighed.

'It's complicated...'

We were at a set of lights, waiting to filter right off the Kantstrasse: Mustapha's was just around the corner.

'Come on, I haven't long left...' I hadn't a clue.

'I am a political refugee, Germany's policy is very helpful, if you can get here.'

I was none the wiser. The taxi was pulling to a halt in front of the restaurant. I thought I'd try an outlandish guess: some far flung Soviet Republic on the Islamic fringe.

'Krzygystan.' I stumbled over the name. ' It's Krzygystan, isn't it?'

He shook his head, smiled ruefully;

'No, no it's not.'

'How much?' I asked, I couldn't see the meter.'

'12 marks, OK?'

'It's ok with me, he's paying.'

I nudged Doc awake and gave him the good news. He handed over the cash. Doc was half-way through the restaurant door. I tapped on the driver's window.

'OK, where are you from?'

'Kosovo.' A catch in his voice.

'What's that? Is it even a country? I've never heard of it.'

'You will,' he said. 'You will.'

9

The Infinite Scope of Memory

Pass me my mnemo-scope,

careful! It's versatile .

Put it to your mind's eye;

it's all the scopes –

from micro to tele –

from minutiae to mediation.

Which one is it,

today?

Like all good scopes

we use it to spy

on the 'other'.

Here, let's gather

intelligence

- on that other

country: the past .

FROM THE REPORT: 'How Could Matthias Rust Get to Moscow?'

BY:　　　　Douglas Clarke, Radio Free Europe

DATE:　　　　1987-6-2

In both the East and the West, people are asking how it could have been possible for a young West German student

pilot, Matthias Rust, to fly a light air-craft unhindered through the vaunted Soviet air defenses.

"It's all a game." Dennis R, 1978 - 2010.

1. Microscope

It's a grubby, cloudy slide under the scope .

It looked like any large institution's open-plan office – except for the radio-electronic hardware. A really close look would tell you it wasn't a standard computer room; oh yes , there *were* huge tape disks and servers the size of small vehicles . But the detail of the missing punch card machines would give it away. I remember the clouds . Of dense, aromatic tobacco smoke; Lambert and Butler, Bensons, - Gauloise for the pretentious few. Everyone smoked then.

Tax-free in the NAAFI, why not? One 23 year old guy affected a meerschaum; he did look like the keyboard player from Sparks, though. It was a big room to fill with smoke. You could barely see the terminal in front of you. A hideous brown block of metal, green-screened with a lighter green font; Zenith Data Systems on a silver metal plate on the side.

It might have been a weekend. Empty seats everywhere you looked: just a few glum faces in the murk. The rest were enjoying 'Stand-downs'; gash time off in honour of the Soviet holiday, 28th of May, Border Guard Day. We had no pilots to listen to. The Soviet Tactical Air Force in the German Democratic Republic was having a well-earned rest; the pilots drinking vodka, the ground crews siphoning fuel tanks to brew white lightning .

How did we know this? We listened: we monitored Soviet radio transmissions; we heard occasional drunken radio checks on common communications frequencies, streams of slurred words demonstrating the rich variety of Russian expletives. Every Soviet holiday was the same; for us as well as them.

The smoke – and the constantly flickering fluorescent lighting – was hard on the eyes. There were no windows in the top-secret listening station. Top Secret! I remember once seeing its phallic lines on the front page of the Sun during Geoffrey Prime's treason trial; a year later I was working in it. No real work to do; what *did* we do that day? Change the slide; turn the knob; focus on the specimen .

Most likely I was listening to a 3-week old recording of a trainee helicopter pilot making landing after landing at an airfield north of Berlin; tapping Cyrillic keys as fast as I could. There were always recordings left over to listen to: we filled databases for faceless bean counters countries away. It would have been about five p.m. Unofficially, our shift had started a quarter of an hour ago, you had to takeover the reins from the off-going crew. You came in a quarter-hour earlier for a 30-second summary and a scrawled note. The hard core would just have been putting their headphones on:

'The shift starts at five, ok? I'll start at five.' Little victories. All they had while in uniform. I never saw the point .

Jock rolled his eyes at me; six hours of head-melting boredom in prospect. He used to string out the administrative duties as long as he could, putting off the donning of the electric hat as long as possible. And he had a hangover; he always did, then. The white noise and static bursts on the cassette recordings made it worse. Twenty years later, we all flinch at loud noises and fail to hear the quiet ones .

At this time the transcription desks would have looked like a '70s school language lab, right down to the empty seats . Eddie had a lurid paperback an inch from his nose and one headset earpiece wedged on the top of his head as far from his good ear as possible. Steve had his feet up beside the desktop control box for his cassette player.

Someone would have made a coffee - for the dozen or so people there - before half-an-hour was out. The TV room-cum-kitchen was in the basement. Big Paul McGill disappeared for over an hour once just to make six brews: but then he did once go AWOL for three days to work as a labourer on a building site . We all pretended not to see him as we drove past the Teufelseestrasse S-Bahn station, on our way to work in the Prick in the Sky.

I would have been working at Teufelsberg for five years - off and on - by then. Some took it very seriously: I did too. Only now does the absurdity of it all hit home. You need memory's lenses to look at the past: the microscope inflates it, the reversed telescope tells the truth; the past is always smaller, sharpened by distance.

2. epocseleT

See me: thinner, younger, smiling less. I run to a bench of radio receivers all set to loudspeaker, a lot of talking; agitated, guttural Russian. It should be brief, hourly checks, drunk or not. Do I hear panic over the ether? Someone has let the tape recordings run out. No-one panics in the room. I don't know what the disembodied voices said. Gone for ever now. Shrugs all round. Good job the Boss Man has taken a rare stand-down.

'Dinnae worry' says Jock 'It'll no be the Red Horde heading for London.'

'We'll never know now, will we?' I muse.

'Who cares who wins?' snorts Steve. Steve's dad is the Boss Man on one of the other shifts.

Jock tells me to reload all the cassette recorders in the room, five racks of 16 plus some 8 individual recorders at another listening station; unmanned because 'we've been recording them'. We man-up all the so-called 24-hour posts. The frequencies we monitor are active for a half-hour or so. It transpires the Soviets want to scramble some assets: the responses are vague and evasive: and quite, quite slurred. Things go back to normal. Their periodic radio checks become flat, atonal, perfunctory. An air of anticlimax spreads to the listeners from the listened-to.

Two more guys come in. In cricket whites, a beer or two to the good after the match. Sport is good for morale. They've heard the boss isn't in. They'll hide in the bogs at shift change and skip out of the building having cheated the Queen of the uniform for an evening. Little, little victories. They are the highest ranked people in the room.

Hours later, I'm nodding off. Back in the 'Language Lab' again. Auditory fancies coming through the headphones; helicopters landing by elephants - or landed by them. My head jerks spastically, tape-recording whiplash injury imminent. Someone's shouting:

'Hurry, downstairs! Come on, the telly.'

Hauling myself from my seat, as if I can't bear to leave my vitally important work - it wouldn't do for anyone to know I've slept through most of a C60 cassette, after all – I follow the crowd down to the TV room...

3. Kaleidoscope

Where it was deathly quiet, except for the sound from the TV. In those pre-satellite days there was no rolling news; no buzz bars ticker-taped world events at the bottom of the screen. The nightly news was on ZDF, with the usual impossibly glamorous, slightly S & M, pastel-power-dresser linking the stories: we strained to follow the newscast German:

'19 year old Mattias Rust landed his Cessna light aircraft in Red Square earlier today...'

I looked round at the faces; Steve, Jock, Paul, the Cricketers: there must have been others – or were others, not these, actually there? Shift the tube and the patterns look different. A few months ago, in Fuengirola, a 50-something man told me he'd sat next to me on the back row of the 'Language Lab' for six months; I didn't even recognise his name.

So, perhaps, Steve sniggered. Maybe Jock's face was unreadable. I know I felt sick. It was too near shift change to call in the stood-down personnel. And what good would it have done?

'Rust departed Finland and crossed into Soviet controlled Airspace before entering Soviet Territory 160 kilometres west of Leningrad...'

Jock shrugged:

'We cannae hear that from here... It's no our responsibility.'

In my head, I was translating his words into Russian.

FROM THE REPORT: 'How Could Matthias Rust Get to Moscow?'

BY: Douglas Clarke, Radio Free Europe

DATE: 1987-6-21

This dramatic incident has caused the dismissal of the head of the Soviet Air Defense Forces and the forced retirement of the Soviet Minister of Defence. Soviet embarrassment over Rust's choice of a landing spot - in Moscow's Red Square - might have been a factor in the severity of the official reaction.

"Nobody really *knows* anything" Ewan Lawrie, October 1989.

10

Denial

ANOTHER COOL, CYPRESS-CYPRUS NIGHT: nothing to hear but the dynamo hum of the insects; nothing to see but the indigo sky dominated by Orion overhead. We were sitting on the veranda, Jock and I. In two mismatched armchairs next to an industrial-sized water cooler. It was 2 a.m. – 0200 local, if you like. Jock's cerulean eyes were shiny with a tamazepam glaze.

Years ago, Bomber Command crews took bennies to stay awake during night missions; we had taken tranks to get to sleep before an early start: progress.

Jock had his nose in a book, his lips moving from time to time; maybe the words meant a lot to him, maybe they meant more if he did that.

'This is a long way from the Ku'damm...' I wanted to talk.

'Yep,' Jock didn't. At least not to me. Not nowadays.

A Land Rover with RAF police markings rumbled past: doing a sweep of the storm drains for drunken airmen. They were too early by an hour or two.

'D'you remember when Dave..?' I persisted, sick of the noise of the bugs.

'Actually I dinnae.' He seemed annoyed. 'You oughtae remember that was aw 20 years ago, for me.' And he had a point, it was: I'd been there longer. I remembered his time there 'though, and, sure, the memory-film slipped in the sprockets, the monochrome was faded and scratched; but, you know, that happens to films when they're played too often.

'Come on, Jock... you must remember something.' I was a bit annoyed myself.

'It's aw a bit o' a blur tae be honest, ye know how it was... so no I dinnae.'

How could he forget? I didn't know. The Mediterranean receded as my mind's eye zoomed out. A jump cut to the 94 bushaltestelle; nine on a late January morning: waiting for the bus to the city. Jock, me, Paddy: Dave was on restrictions, washing pint glasses in the Officers' Mess kitchen; Dave got caught for anything and everything. All of us were a little bleary, weary: first days-off in the shift cycle, we were up early, after a night in the NAAFI.

'This is just the best, you know,' Paddy's cultured tones filled with enthusiasm. 'Grünewoche, I mean.'

Grünewoche – one of the few words every Brit in Berlin managed to learn. Greenweek it meant.

'I can't wait to see the fresians!' he went on.

'Like you'll even see the livestock hall!' I jeered.

And the truth was none of us would. Greenweek was Berlin's annual agricultural show. Produce from all over

the world on show in the Messege-
lande: West Berlin's futuristic exhibition centre: Guinness, Elephant Beer,
Tiger Beer, Fosters, Amstel, scotch
and Irish whiskey, aquavit, vodka.

Phil, long gone, had seen the fresians
one year: demonstrating an alarming
lack of skill in the art of rodeo - before
being arrested by the Berlin Police,
who handcuffed him to a lamppost
out front, while they waited for the
MPs.

Jock stumbled as we got off the bus
near the Funkturm, West Berlin's radio tower: a mini Eiffel dwarfed by
its uglier East German version on the
other side of the wall.

'Steady,' said Paddy. 'We haven't started yet!'

'Had a few swallies in the room, after the bar closed. I'm OK'. Jock gave a lopsided grin.

I paid the entry fee for all of us: my round would be later, now. Jock wrote my name on the back of his hand.

'Where first, gentlemen?' Paddy asked, one eyebrow raised à la Roger Moore.

'Ireland. Guinness, come awn!' Jock had perked up a bit.

'No, let's save it: go there later, let's do Weinstrasse.'

I went with the flow: Paddy had wanted to go down Weinstrasse for a couple of years. Two phalanxes of stands dedicated to German vineyards, free samples at every one, if you played your cards right. The owl-like JB had donned a suit and tie one year, suc-

cessfully posing as an Oddbins buy-
er. So well, in fact, that the following
week he was summoned to the guardroom at the main gate to explain the
arrival of 30 cases of hock with his
name on them.

They were more organised nowadays
of course: we'd had no more than 5
free glasses each before we were po-
litely advised to visit other parts of the
exhibition.

'This beer's pish.' Jock avowed.

'It's French, what d'you expect?' Paddy seemed unbothered.

'Better eat something, eh?' I showed
off my schoolboy French to the stun-
ner behind the counter, I just wanted
to hear her speak.

'Qu'est-ce tu veux. Il y a d'huîtres, tres
bien!'

'Oui, bien sûr!' So suave.

'I love those French birds.' I announced: 'they have a certain Je ne sais pas.' As it turned out that was me: the oysters arrived.

'Mmm, lovely.' I bluffed it out.

'Wha' the fuck are thon?' Jock was horrified.

'You mean you don't know?' An incredulous Paddy.

'Really nice – gulp!' It was getting harder to keep it up, or the oysters down. 'Go on, have one.'

Jock picked up the shell, carefully, finger-and-thumb, trying to reconcile keeping it at arm's length with putting the oyster in his mouth.

'That's it, just gulp it down!'

'Arrrrrrrrrrrgh!' The oyster trampolined across the counter, Mam'selle ducked for cover behind it, a hair finally out of place.

'It's fuckin' snotters, ye bastards!' Jock bellowed. We headed for Denmark, for blondes and Elephant Beer, Ireland was next door.

'More pish! When do we get shum deshent beer?'

'Jock, it's decent enough by the sound of you!' Paddy grinned.

'It is nearly six percent proof, Jock, is that not strong enough?'

It patently was.

'Aye, it's no that, just the taste, ye ken?, I'll see yez next door, awrigh'?'

'OK, keep your eye on him Paddy.' I warned, suspecting Paddy's eye would rather be on Astrid. Ireland was the stand next door, one of the bigger ones naturally. He'd be alright.

'Just two more Astrid, thanks.' Paddy smarmed. I raised my eyes at 5 feet 10 inches of Nordic cliché: got a smile back. Smarm isn't everything.. I liked Elephant beer, stronger than Carlsberg Special Export and probably named for the feeling you got after four; that of being run over by one. I remember daydreaming for a bit, probably fantasising about Astrid, while Paddy kept trying.

Suddenly I heard shouting in an all-too-familiar accent. Ireland had round table tops on tall barrels; a country for standing in. France, of course, had had comfortable chairs. It was still relatively empty in Ireland: only Jock sprawled across a table with his hands locked around the throat of a soutaned priest.

'Better go, Paddy', I said.

I jerked my head over the border, threw 20 deutschmarks on the counter. Astrid stared open-mouthed toward the drama in the other bar.

Paddy had Jock by the scruff of the neck: I asked the Priest:

'What's that all about, Father? Can I get you a drink?'

' No, I am fine... I was in here just, well, it's the Irish stand... A Guinness, a chat, you know...'

'Yeah, well we all get homesick, sometimes. So what was it?'

'A conversation, only, about celibacy: it was fine, I told him what he wanted to know. Then he asked about masturbation... I told him the sin of Onan was between him and his god. Deuteronomy forbids it, you know.'

As it happened I did.

Jock didn't, it appeared:

'Tell 'um. Paddy, I'll no be spoken tae like tha'

We took him away, to explain it to him, while the 94 bus rumbled over the S-Bahn tracks crossing the Heerstrasse...

And Berlin faded out, as the diesel-rattle of the crew bus went down to idle. Jock put his bible in the leg-pocket of his flying suit.

'You really don't remember?' I asked for the third time.

'No.' he said, succinct, precise, accentless. 'I don't.'

I wondered if he could hear the sound of the cock crowing in the distance.

11

A Drink After Work

P ERHAPS YOU'D READ ON if I wrote this in the present tense. More immediate, more visceral. Tough; it all happened a long time ago. Microscope with the present and you'll get the detail, but you'll miss the picture.

Friday was on my mind, as it happened. Not least because it was; a Friday, that is. Or, more specifically, Friday evening was uppermost in my hungover thoughts. I was hiding in my boss's office. He was hiding behind an almost-lie on the whiteboard in that office. He'd written 'COURSE' in wavering green capitals. The green marker-ink was probably a joke, since it was a Golf Course. Still, we both knew the Russians weren't going to invade that day; they hadn't in forty years and they wouldn't any time soon. Most of us kept that to ourselves.

May Day was Sunday; nobody was going to fly even a tatty old Fishbed before the big parade. All our shift workers would stand down at mid-day. I was going to stay until four in the afternoon. 16.00 hours local, out loud. The price of a day job. Besides, I had graphs to draw, sorties to count, trends to identify: a monumental waste of time, ever since a few free-spirited Berliners had danced atop the wall, sounding the beat with sledgehammers. Still, it didn't do to say you were wasting your time, although that's what military life is, away from the battlefield. Especially in intelligence.

At about 15.45, Jock poked his head around the door,

'Beer on the way home?' He winked.

'Home? Let's just go for a beer.'

After the IRA attacks 'down the zone', as we still called West Germany, we had to travel to and from the 'Berg in civvies. This edict had gained us all a usable locker after twenty years of cramming things into something the size of a shoe-box. I shut down the computer, and its outmoded green screen took its obsolescent time about winking out. Jock and I were changed and out the door at 16.00 on the dot. Military time-keeping is a habit. We scrounged a lift down the 'Berg with a USAF Sergeant he knew from the last Anglo-American Friendship Day. We learned quite a bit about Joseph Smith, before leaping out of the car at the S-Bahn station on the corner of the Heerstraße.

'Kaiser Friedrich?' I asked.

'Mons.' Jock said.

'Not again.'

We went. Late afternoon was a good time to talk to the girls. Business was slow, there was only a desultory effort at doing the show. Even Mme Stradivarius' fiddling was unaccompanied by any chorally simulated orgasm. The beers came, Charlottenburger Pils. Possibly the worst brew in Berlin.

I lifted my glass,

'To the Free World,' I said.

'Fuck 'em,' Jock said.

12

The Spy Who Was Mince*

O F COURSE WE weren't. Spies, I mean. Hometown friends got the wrong end of the stick, that's all. Positive Vetting. PV. That's what it was called then. After "they" had checked back three generations for Reds Under The Bed or secret Oswald Mosley fans, people going into "sensitive" jobs had to give two character referees, sometimes three. Those sensitive jobs could be at Cheltenham, Scarborough or perhaps Harrogate, if you were going into the Civil Service. Going into the RAF was quite different. If you were wise – or just plain lucky – you chose people who knew you well enough to know which lies to commit by omission. I did. I chose rugby people.

Just 18 months after those lies were told, I was in West Berlin. You couldn't tell anyone, not even your parents, what you were doing. My dad had served 31 years, from Palestine to Catterick and lots of stops in between. "They" liked "service issue", I always used to say. It made them think they knew what they were getting.

An officer in charge of one of the shifts – just before they decided we only needed one between two of four shift teams – once said we were all a bunch of oddball and misfit "phrase- ologists", which example of man- agement insight only proved that we didn't need officers at all, at least not on shift. Which fact they caught on to quite quickly – for officers – and thereafter we only saw them on our two day shifts in the rota.

We worked in a listening post. You may have heard of it (Boom! Boom!) It was called Teufelsberg – Devil's Mountain – although it wasn't much more than a hill. The Americans had bulldozed a load of bombed-out Berlin rubble into a hill just after the war. I suppose for a few years it was just a hut and an antenna.

Our little unit was nested like a Russ- ian doll inside Field Station Berlin, the official name for Teufelsberg. I think there might have been 300 UK personnel in total, in '85 or so. About 200 would have been linguists, like me. Back on the RAF station that was our parent unit, there was a large former Hangar where the other signals and telemetry were collected. When I first stepped through the doors into the set-room "up the hill" a couple of years earlier, these men and women worked there too.

There was a shift bus from RAF Gatow to T'Berg (and yeah, we did have fun, fun, fun 'til the baddies took our T'berg away, thanks). However, almost everyone drove up in the tax-free car we each bought when we finally realised our only money problem was how to spend it all. I used to get the shift bus if I'd had a heavy night between evenings and days, or days and days, or if I happened to forget to stop drinking early enough before the night shift.

So all the intelligence collected – nobody called it intel then, not even the Yanks – was sifted and analysed and reported on right up until sometime in '92, not long after I left. Of course, it turned out that the Soviet weaponry was not quite so efficient as some of the reports might have indicated. Even so, 'probable' indicates only a >50% likelihood of something happening and that, my friends, is a 49.99999*% likelihood of something not happening. Think Iraqi chemical weapons and you'll figure out the culprits for that lie **and** the duration of the Cold War. The wheel of fortune has turned again. I have a few former colleagues who must be very busy now.

Call me a spy if you like, but none of us were mince, not really.

*Mince: Scottish vernacular for really not very good.

13

Dreizehn

THOUGH I WAS PRAYING he wouldn't, the fat, drunk guy sat down next to me. Four tables on about 5 square metres of pavement outside the *kneipe* and a guy with a waistline that dwarfed the circumference of the table tops stumbled into a chair, opposite me. I saved my beer and my wife's too. The other guy at the table wasn't so lucky. There was a bottle of something blue in the behemoth's hand. I thought it was an alcopop, but it was just funny-coloured spring water. Every other person on the *"terasse"* wished him "Good Evening" in the way that Berliners would, even if your trousers were round your ankles and you had been sick in them.

Dreizehn was in Schöneburg, on the corner of Fuggerstrasse. It might have been named after the number in its address on Welzerstrasse, but it wasn't. Being in Schöneburg it catered for a specific clientele. It was cheap and it was open. Besides, all the joints, in all the towns, in all the world can't afford to turn paying customers away. Not nowadays. There was no-one under 40 there. When we'd arrived there were smiles of welcome. Berlin has always been a live-and-let-live kind of place.

I went inside to order more drinks, Vince and Andy were on the music system. No doubt Jimmy would be on later whether in Bronski Beat or The Communards. The barman was in lederhosen. Yep, just lederhosen, nothing else. Still, it had been a hot day. I paid for the drinks and left a 2 euro tip. Well, the drinks were cheap, as I said. I took the beers outside.

The big man started singing. Everybody laughed. The songs, or the brief excerpts from songs, were all rude. The other guy at our table asked him to sing the DDR's national anthem. He didn't think it was funny. Both guys referred to themselves as "*Osis*", and they didn't mean Australians. The slim guy at our table had fled the East in 1986, illegally.

'I wish I had waited 3 years, until the wall fell down. It was hard in West

Berlin for illegals in that time. Also, Bowie had gone by then.'

The big fellow had actually been quiet for a bit. I'd thought he'd fallen asleep. We all jumped when he shouted, 'Do you know where I was, in '86?'

Well, of course, we didn't, but I knew we were about to find out, and probably at some length. Anyway, this is more or less what he said, minus some of the digressions, repetition and pointing of fingers.

'I was a career soldier, you know. In the NVA, the Nationale Volksarmee. A career soldier. I did not work on the border, nein, never on the border. I trained the conscripts. So you know, I was a professional soldier. And now I drive a bus. A fucking bus.'

At this point, perhaps unwisely, I said, "in 86 I was here, in Berlin."

'24th April 1986. You know what happened then, huh? Yes, that's right the big fuck up.'

He took a sip out the bottle, dainty in the way some really obese men are.

'On April 25th, we got on two buses, me, a gefreiter or two and 100 conscripts. I asked the Leutnant where we were going. He said it was top secret. But it wasn't long before we saw the signposts pointing towards the Polish border. Soon we were in Frankfurt, our Frankfurt, on the Oder river. The buses parked outside the Grenzbahhnof, the Border Railway Station. The Leutnant told me to line all the men up for inspection and a few words. He was a short man. Always in dress uniform, never in fatigues or battledress. Perhaps he knew how he'd look in them. Doubtless

he was unhappy at the dust on his shoes as he stood outside the Railway Station. I brought the men to attention. The Leutnant walked along the first rank, picked a bit of lint from the shoulder of one man, asked another when he'd last shaved. I could see his heart wasn't in it. He stalked off, stood on the steps leading into the station and told me to stand the men at ease. I was expecting a long speech. Like most officers he liked the sound of his own voice.

This time he didn't speak for any longer than it took to tell us our mission was most important, for the safety and security of the Deutsche Demokratische Republic, and that we must never tell anyone about it. He gave a salute, and walked off. I stood the men to attention just in time to give him a salute. I was about to march the men around for something to do, when the Leutnant bellowed "Sergeant Fuchs!"'

He was standing to the rear of one of the buses smoking an American cigarette. They smelled different. The officers could always get contraband. He blew out a long plume of smoke.,

"Take them to the far end of the building Sergeant, you are looking for the shunting yard".

'So that was what I did. Some uniformed railway employee was waiting for us. There were dozens of trains, passenger and freight. Cyrillic writing on some of them. Every line was full. The man was standing in front of a huge bowser, marked for hazardous chemicals. 3 or 4 hoses were attached to the outpipes,There were around a 100 stiff brushes leaning against a wall, in serried ranks like the soldiers who were to use them.

'"Clean them," the Railway man said, pointing at the rolling stock. "Clean them

all." Then he handed me a large sack, full of paper masks, like the Japanese wear nowadays, in their polluted cities.

'So we hosed and scrubbed all day and half of the night. I counted 48 trains. Then they started to move them out. When the last one had gone, the lines began to fill again. But I knocked the men off. We hadn't even eaten. I hunted for the Leutnant, but he was nowhere to be found. After I grabbed the Railway Official by the throat, he agreed to bring some food out from the official canteen. I told him there had better be some beer or I'd tear his arms off and feed him the soggy ends. We got some soup and some very hard bread. Then we slept on the buses. It was like that for four days. By the time we'd finished the rumours about Chernobyl were everywhere. When the last train pulled out the Leutnant finally appeared in his pressed uniform and shiny shoes.

"Let's go, Sergeant," he said.

'Like most people I slept all the way back to the barracks in the bus. Of course it was the same rigmarole when we arrived. Parade the men, a cursory inspection and a few words from the Leutnant. When he finished I gave the command "Officer on Parade, dismiss". The men executed slovenly salutes followed by worse quarter turns and fell out. The Leutnant leaned back to look up at me,*

"Well done, Sergeant," he said.

'Four years later the Peoples's Army was disbanded, just like that. Minute pensions, tens of thousands of career soldiers on the streets. I heard the Leutnant died of cancer, guess avoiding the trains didn't help.'*

The fat man seemed sober now. A seat became free at the table alongside, and he took it. I took a long sip of beer. It was good beer, too.

Afterword

Madame Stradivarius, or Birgitte, is an MEP for the Greens representing the NeuBrandenburg Region.

Dave is married with 2.4 children.

Jock has found God, although he says God found him. I'm surprised he was looking.

Ute married a former Neo-Nazi in a civil ceremony in 2007.

Jurgen 'retired' to Majorca, got bored, opened a club and sold it for a lot of dollars which a Russian delivered in a suitcase one dark night.

Nada married a Somalian refugee and is a campaigner for refugees' rights in Germany.

Phil runs a taxi business in a town in East Anglia.

Julischka disappeared while on holiday in Kos in 1991. Her ex-husband was in jail at the time.

Doc is not Jock, despite being Scottish. He survived a bout of cancer and works for the BBC.

Kurt lives in Majorca, possibly with Jurgen.

Mustapha's restaurant is now a laundrette. I hope Mustapha's taxi is for hire in Pristina, but I doubt it.

Eddie made a pile of money and spends his life on holiday.

Steve is a senior officer in the RAF. I hope he's happy anyway.

Paul is a TEFL teacher in the Far East, I think he might do some DIY building on the side.

The Cricketers are in the Members' Bar in the Sky.

There were actually two **Paddy**s: one is very high up in a world of diplomats and spies; the other, I suppose, is still alarming women when drunk, by making faces at them.

Mon Cheri's and **The Elephant Bar** are still open for business during the late hours in Charlottenburg. The girls have been Asian and are now, mostly, Eastern European. The beer is better though.

And **me**? I make things up, but you know that, don't you?

Printed in Great Britain
by Amazon